PUPPY PALS

Bailey

SUSAN HUGHES

sourcebooks
jabberwocky

Published by Sourcebooks Jabberwocky, an imprint of Sourcebooks, Inc.
P.O. Box 4410, Naperville, Illinois 60567-4410
(630) 961-3900
Fax: (630) 961-2168
www.sourcebooks.com

Originally published as Bailey's Visit in 2013 in Canada by Scholastic Canada Ltd.

Library of Congress Cataloging-in-Publication data is on file with the publisher.

Source of Production: Versa Press, East Peoria, Illinois, USA
Date of Production: March 2016
Run Number: 5006164

Printed and bound in the United States of America.
VP 10 9 8 7 6 5 4 3 2 1

For my sister-in-law, Carolyne Hughes,

and her spaniel pals, Bella and Hailey

uppies were running across the grass. Dozens of puppies.

Some were black, some were brown, and some were white with black spots. Some puppies were red and shaggy, and some were gray with white muzzles. All the puppies had smiling faces and wagging tails.

Kat was sitting on her front steps. Her eyes were closed. She was having her favorite puppy daydream. And it always ended the same…

The puppies jump around, begging for her attention. Her mother and father smile at her.

"Of course you can have a puppy, Katherine," her mom says.

Her dad sweeps out his arm. "Pick any one you want!"

Kat smiles too. She looks at all the puppies, and she tries to choose. The little toffee-colored Irish terrier that jumps into her lap? The shy gray schnauzer looking at her, his head cocked to one side? The black pug so tiny that—

Aidan's running shoe nudged her leg, and Kat opened her eyes. As usual, her brother was listening to music. He pulled out one of his earbuds. "Come on, Kat," he said. "Let's go! We're going to be late for school."

Kat sighed. The daydream was over. She sent a mental message to the puppies: I'll come back and visit soon!

She ran to catch up with Aidan. The sun was shining. A squirrel chattered at her from the branch of a chestnut tree.

"Do you think Mom and Dad will ever let me get a dog?" Kat asked her brother as they walked.

Aidan shrugged. "You've asked them a million times. They always say no."

"That's because they travel so much for work. But I don't!" Kat protested. "And *I'd* be the one looking after the dog."

Aidan bounced his basketball as he walked. "I don't know, Kat. I think you should forget about it for now."

Kat sighed. She knew he would say that. He didn't care if they got a dog or not. Her parents both liked dogs, but she was the only one who was truly dog crazy.

Kat and Aidan reached school just as the bell rang.

"Later, alligator," Aidan said to Kat. He hurried over to the seventh- and eighth-grade entrance.

"See you soon, baboon!" Kat called after him.

She rushed across the playground. But she didn't get in her line. Instead, Kat went over to the other fourth-grade line.

"Maya!" she called. Her best friend hung back as her class made its way into the school.

"There you are, Kat-Nip! Late again!" Maya said with a grin.

Kat made a funny face back at her. Maya had called her "Kat-Nip" for as long as she could remember. "You love dogs, but your name is Kat? How goofy!" she'd say. Maya often teased her, and Kat teased her back.

It was all in fun, since they had been best friends forever. Even though they lived on opposite sides of town, they had known each other since nursery school. They played soccer on the same team. They took swimming lessons together. Most of all, they talked about dogs together. Maya was probably the only person in the world who loved dogs as much as Kat.

Until this year, Maya and Kat had always been in the same class. But a few children had moved away over the summer. So Maya was put in the other fourth-grade class.

The girls didn't like it. Not one bit.

School had started last week. The first few days had been tough. Kat hoped it would be better this week, but it didn't seem likely.

"Joke of the day: what does a mother dog call

her pups when they come in from playing in the snow?" Kat asked.

Maya thought for a moment. "I don't know. What?"

"I'll tell you at recess!" Kat said, waggling her fingertips at her friend. She turned to run toward her lineup.

"Hey, not fair! Tell me now!" called Maya. "That's torture!"

"Nope! Oh, and I have some really awesome news to tell you," Kat called over her shoulder. "Puppy news!" she added, taunting her friend.

"Seriously? And you won't tell me what it is until recess? You are horrible!" Maya put on her grumpy look, but she couldn't hold it for long. Kat started to laugh, and Maya did too.

"See you!" Kat teased. She ran to the back of her own line that had just disappeared into the school.

CHAPTER 2

"So?" Maya asked, running up to Kat at recess. "What does a mother dog call her pups when they come in from playing in the snow?"

Kat grinned. "The answer? Drumroll, please... Slush puppies!"

"Agh!" Maya groaned. She pretended to throw a tennis ball at Kat. "Take that!"

Kat caught the ball easily and laughed out loud. She loved telling jokes to Maya. Her friend always responded dramatically, either loving the joke or hating it. She tossed the ball back to Maya. They threw it back and forth a few more times.

"Okay, next—the puppy news. What is it?" Maya called.

Kat threw the ball back to her, but her aim was wide. "Oops!"

The ball flew past Maya and onto the field. It landed right in the middle of some boys who were tossing a football around.

"Uh-oh," Kat said. She went to stand beside Maya.

Then Kat saw Megan and Cora, two girls in her class, pointing at her. They were giggling.

"Nice, Kat," Megan called. "Did you do that on purpose?"

"Do you want to play with your boyfriend?" teased Cora.

"Oh, great," moaned Kat.

"It's your own fault, klutz," said Maya, poking her elbow into Kat's side. "You'd better go get it."

"No way." Kat shook her head. "Not alone."

"Come on. We'll ask your *boyfriend* to give it back to us," said Maya, grabbing Kat's arm and heading toward the field.

"Very funny," said Kat. She didn't have a boyfriend, and Maya knew it. But for some reason, Owen, one of the boys, seemed to get all tongue-tied when Kat was around. Sometimes he chased her when the class played tag.

Maya was certain this meant Owen liked Kat.

It seemed like Megan and Cora thought so too.

But it was Matthew, a boy from Maya's class, who picked up their tennis ball.

As Maya marched Kat toward him, he tossed the ball up and down in his hand.

"Thanks, Matthew," Maya said. "Can you throw it back to us?"

Matthew grinned. He threw it to his buddy Sunjit.

"Sunjit," Kat said. She held out her hands. "Over here. Please?"

"Sure thing," Sunjit said. He tossed the ball to Owen.

Maya and Kat stopped. They both frowned.

"Funny," Maya said.

"So hilarious," Kat added. Owen blushed. He froze looking at them.

Maya nudged Kat again. "Basset hound," she whispered.

This was one of the girls' favorite games.

They would name a dog breed that a person reminded them of. For example, Kat thought Maya was like an English setter. Elegant. Graceful. Loyal.

Kat looked at Owen. A basset hound? Yes, she could see it. She began to giggle. Until

Maya softly cooed, "Oh, look at that face. Those lovey-dovey eyes!"

Ugh. No!

"Come on, Owen," yelled Matthew. "Over here. What are you waiting for?"

Owen shrugged and threw the ball to Kat.

"Not back to *them*," Sunjit groaned, smacking his forehead with the palm of his hand.

Maya and Kat laughed and ran back to where they'd been tossing the ball back and forth.

Cora and Megan were still giggling and whispering, but Kat tried to ignore them.

"Okay, finally. The puppy news," Maya said. "Spill it. I need to know now!"

And just then, the bell rang.

"Line up, please, students!" called the teacher on yard duty. "No dawdling! To your lines!"

With a moan, Maya grabbed her hair and pulled at it. "I live a life of torment!" she exclaimed.

Kat giggled. Maya would make a great actress! The girls headed toward the school.

"Okay, okay," Kat said quickly. "Remember

I told you my aunt Jenn was opening a dog-grooming salon?"

"Of course, I remember," Maya replied, rolling her eyes.

"Lines, students! Get in your lines!" the teacher shouted again.

"Well, it's opening today! Aunt Jenn called to let us know last night," explained Kat. "My mom and dad are going to finish work early, so we can go and see her place after school. And they said you can come with us. If you want."

"That's so cool! We can ask my mom at lunch." Maya looked excited. The girls took turns going to each other's houses at lunchtime. Today it was Kat's turn to go to Maya's house.

"Miss Reynolds? Do you have somewhere

you need to be?" It was the recess-duty teacher. She looked at Kat pointedly.

"Right. See you, Maya," Kat said, and off she hurried. She couldn't wait until this afternoon!

CHAPTER 3

There it is! Aunt Jenn's place: Tails Up! Boarding and Grooming," cried Kat, reading the sign.

She and Maya ran ahead of the rest of the family, past the barber shop, the bank, and the hardware store. Then they waited impatiently for everyone to catch up.

Kat's father, Mr. Reynolds, frowned as he came up and read a sign in the store window. "*Walk-ins are welcome.* Don't most dogs walk in?" he asked. "Though, I guess some dogs might have dirty paws, so carrying them in would be better."

"Funny, Dad." Kat grinned. "You know it means that people don't have to make appointments ahead of time. They can just walk in with their dogs."

"Oh, yeah. Right," Mr. Reynolds said, grinning back at her.

But then he frowned for real. "I just hope Jenn can handle it all. Your aunt is a very enthusiastic person—especially when it comes to dogs. I love her dearly. But sometimes she can get a bit carried away with her projects."

"Oh, Robert," said Mrs. Reynolds. "You worry too much about your sister! I'm sure she'll be fine. Come on, gang. Let's go in."

"Yeah, let's go," said Kat. She and Maya led the way into Tails Up!

The waiting room had a small couch and three chairs. There was a scale and shelves lined with bags of dog food. At the front desk was a computer, a cash register, and a phone.

There were two customers waiting in the little room. One was a young man who sat with a white shih tzu on his lap. The other was a woman with a long-haired Shetland sheepdog lying at her feet. Both customers looked impatient.

Just then, Aunt Jenn came flying out of a room in the back. She wore a white grooming coat. Her brown hair was mostly pulled back in a ponytail. A few stray hairs frizzed around her forehead. With her was a thin man holding a tiny Chihuahua.

"So how was she?" the man asked nervously. "It was Chiquita's first time being groomed."

"She was a natural. Very calm," Aunt Jenn said. "It was a pleasure to groom her."

The man smiled, relieved. He quickly paid his bill and left.

"And now, hello to you, my loyal family!" Aunt Jenn cried, hurrying toward them with her arms open. She gave each family member a huge hug. "Hello, my Kitty-Kat," she said. That was her special name for Kat. She lifted Kat right off her feet!

Then she turned to Maya. "And my most-special niece's most-special friend, you came too!" And Maya was swept up in a hug as well.

"The place looks fantastic!" Mrs. Reynolds said.

"Yes, well done," Mr. Reynolds added. Aunt Jenn plastered a kiss on his cheek. He patted her on the back awkwardly.

"Oh, it is so nice to have a fan club," Aunt Jenn said, pleased. "Would you all like a tour? This, of course, is the reception area," she said, throwing her arms wide. "When I get a receptionist, this is where she or he will sit."

Mr. Reynolds looked worried. "You haven't hired any help yet?"

Mrs. Reynolds poked him. But Aunt Jenn answered cheerfully, "Nope. Can't quite afford it yet."

"Um, excuse me." It was the woman with the sheltie. She was standing now. "I'm Mrs. Fennel, and I have been waiting for quite some time. I believe my Clarke-Davis is next to be groomed."

Aunt Jenn ruffled her brother's hair. "Oh, Mrs. Fennel," she said. "You don't think this shaggy guy needs some emergency attention?"

Kat and Maya giggled.

Mrs. Fennel frowned. "Oh, well," she stammered. "No, I meant…"

"Your sheltie is beautiful," Kat said quickly. "What's his name?"

Mrs. Fennel's frown vanished. Her face lit up. "Why, thank you. His name is Clarke-Davis."

Clarke-Davis? Kat tried not to giggle again. "I love dogs," she said. "May I pet him?"

"Certainly," the woman replied, pleased.

Kat knelt beside the brown-and-white dog. Gently, she ran her hand over his back. "His hair is so soft," she exclaimed.

"Well, I brush him twice a week. And then I

have him clipped once a month." The woman turned to Aunt Jenn. "My old groomer moved away last month. I was hoping you might be as good as him, although it's doubtful. No one, no one has ever had a way with Clarke-Davis like Roberto did."

"And what about us?" It was the young man

with the shih tzu in his lap. His dog was asleep, but he wasn't.

"Mr. Winston, you're welcome to leave Clyde here until I'm ready for him," suggested Aunt Jenn. "I have several crates in the back room. He'd be quite comfortable there while he waits, and then you don't need to sit here with him."

"Leave Clyde in a crate?" The man looked horrified. "Never."

"Well, we'll just be a second," explained Aunt Jenn. "Promise."

She pointed to the room that she'd just come out of. "My grooming room."

Kat peeked in. She saw two large grooming tables and two stand dryers. Several grooming brushes, clippers, shavers, shampoo bottles, and other equipment were scattered nearby.

Aunt Jenn opened a door to another large room with windows. There were several big crates lined up side by side. "This is where the dogs waiting to be groomed will stay. If their owners will let them!" She winked at Kat. "And the dogs I board will be lodged here as well. I guess I could call it the doggy day care room!"

She pointed to a stairway. "Up there is a large room where I can do some puppy training. And there's a big yard out back that I can use too. So you see? I'm all set!"

"And you're going to live here too?" Kat's father raised his eyebrows.

"Yup. There's another room upstairs that is now officially my bedroom. And there's a small bathroom and kitchen too," said Aunt Jenn.

"Grooming, boarding, training… You're planning to do all of these, Jenn?" Mr. Reynolds asked doubtfully.

"Sure am," Aunt Jenn said confidently, with a toss of her ponytail.

Mrs. Reynolds nudged her husband and turned to his younger sister. "It all looks wonderful," she said firmly.

Aidan pulled out one of his earphones. "Very cool," he agreed, nodding.

"Thanks, Reynolds family!" said Aunt Jenn with a grin.

As Kat's parents and Aidan went back out to the reception room, Aunt Jenn motioned to Kat and Maya to stay behind. "I don't really want your dad to know this yet, Kat," she said quietly. "He'll just think I'm in over my head. But… well, I have a little surprise to show you girls."

Kat and Maya stared at one another. What could it be?

ollow me," said Aunt Jenn. She led them to the far side of the room. A crate sat under the window in the sunshine. But it wasn't empty.

"Oh!" Kat breathed.

"A puppy!" said Maya.

A golden-yellow puppy lay in a corner of the crate all curled up, sleeping peacefully. But he must have heard the girls' voices, because just then he woke up.

He lifted his head and looked at the girls

with his beautiful blue eyes. Then he jumped to his feet and wagged his tail energetically.

Kat's heart melted.

"His name is Bailey," explained Aunt Jenn. "He's a Labrador retriever pup. He's only eight weeks old. His owner, Kelly, has only had him for a few days, but she found out last night that she has to go out of town for three days. There aren't many kennels nearby, and most of them are large. She didn't want to take him to a big kennel. She saw my sign, so she called just this morning to see if I'd take Bailey until she's back." Aunt Jenn shrugged. "Look at him. I just had to say yes!"

Kat looked at the adorable little puppy. She knew exactly what Aunt Jenn meant. That was one of the things she loved about her aunt: she'd do anything to help a dog.

"I'll just have to scoot out here every once in a while to check in on him," said Aunt Jenn. "And then tonight and tomorrow night, I'll bring his crate up to my bedroom. It should be fine." It sounded like Aunt Jenn was trying to convince herself.

"Of course, it'll be fine," Kat said reassuringly. She slipped her arm around Aunt Jenn's waist as they headed back to the front door. "Tails Up! is amazing, Aunt Jenn," said Kat. "And so are you."

"Totally amazing!" said Maya.

"It's like a dream come true, girls," said Aunt Jenn. "Listen, I'm quite busy today—opening day and all—but I'm sure things will settle down by tomorrow. I'll have lots of free time in the days ahead. I'm sure it will take a while for word to get around about my new salon. So feel free to drop by anytime and keep me company. We can chat puppies together."

"Tomorrow, after school? Can we come then?" Kat asked quickly.

"Please?" Maya added.

"Of course," Aunt Jenn said with a smile.

The girls grinned at each other. It was a plan!

CHAPTER 5

The next day, Kat and Maya were at Kat's house for lunch.

"So how's it going in your class?" Kat asked. She dipped a carrot stick in peanut butter and chomped on it.

Maya shrugged. "Not bad. The younger kids are a bit of a pain. And I miss you, of course," she added quickly.

Kat nodded. It was okay. Maya was much more outgoing than she was. Everyone liked Maya, and she made friends quickly. She was probably already good friends with all the girls in her class. Just good friends though. Not best friends. That spot was reserved for Kat.

Maya swallowed a sip of milk. "You?" she asked.

"Megan and Cora are driving me nuts," responded Kat. "They won't stop teasing me. About Owen."

Maya made a face. "He totally likes you, Kat," she said.

Kat rolled her eyes. "No, he doesn't!"

"He's always watching you!" Maya replied.

"Whatever. Anyway, I don't mind when you say stuff like that. You're not trying to be mean. But when Megan and Cora say it, it's different. Irritating. They're trying to get to me. They were like this last year too. But somehow, with you there, it wasn't as bad."

"Well, maybe you need to think of a way of getting back at them," Maya suggested.

"Getting back at them?"

"Yeah, you know. Revenge. Payback," Maya said. "Kat, come on. You don't watch enough bad movies. Don't you know? Revenge can be sweet!"

The girls laughed and finished eating. Then Maya said, "Let's go look at puppies!"

"Yes!" Kat cheered. The girls ran to the family's computer in the living room.

They began drooling over photo after photo of adorable puppies. There were Afghans and Dobermans, Wheaten terriers and huskies, and more! Each one was ridiculously cute.

"If you could have any puppy, what would you pick?" Kat asked Maya. It was the question they always asked each other. What if someday they were allowed to get a dog? They wanted to be ready to choose! But it was so hard. Each time, they gave a different answer.

"Today, I would choose a Bernese mountain dog," Maya replied. She clicked to a photo of a Bernese mountain puppy. His coat was black, white, and rust-colored. He looked as soft as a stuffed animal. "I read that they can be very loving. Some people even train them to pull a cart!"

Maya pushed the mouse to Kat. "How about you?" she asked. "What would you choose?"

"This little guy is my favorite," Kat said, clicking to a standard schnauzer puppy with perky ears and a curly black coat. His eyes sparkled

with mischief. "Schnauzers are very smart. They even work as police and guard dogs."

"He's so cute! But, really, how could we ever choose just one?" Maya sighed. "There are hundreds of dog breeds. And mixed dogs are adorable too!"

"And I always change my mind," Kat said. "Do I want a big dog or a small dog? Do I want a really smart dog or a really loyal one? I'd love a dog that I could pick up and cuddle with. But I also want one to run with at the park. They are all so different!"

"We'll just have to adopt a bunch of dogs then," Maya said, laughing.

That's when Kat got the idea. "Hey, I know!" she said, grabbing Maya's arm. "Let's make a scrapbook. We can call it our Puppy Collection. It will be kind of like having our own puppies right now. We can make a page or two about the puppies we like the most. We can draw pictures—or print out photos— and put them in the scrapbook."

"That's an awesome idea!" Maya said. "And

we can write a description about each one: what the puppy looks like, what it likes to do, what kind of care it needs—things like that!" She was just as excited as Kat.

"We can even name our puppies!" Kat looked nervously at her friend. "Or is that too dumb?"

"No, not dumb. Brilliant again, Einstein!" Maya said with a grin.

"I'll ask my mom tonight if we can buy a scrapbook," Kat said. She couldn't wait!

"I think my mom has some scrapbook supplies at home too." Maya was practically jumping up and down. "Oh, and I have lots of puppy stickers! Let's print out the pictures of today's puppies to get started."

The girls printed out a few pictures and started daydreaming about puppy names.

"What about Schneider for my puppy?" Kat asked.

"Schneider the schnauzer—I love it! It's dignified. It will totally suit his mustache!" Maya said. "What about Bernie for my Bernese mountain dog? Is it too silly?"

"It has personality!" Kat replied. "I think it suits him."

"Hey, are we still planning to go to your aunt's grooming studio after school?" Maya asked.

"Of course," Kat said. "She said we could. Remember?"

Then she sat up straight. She looked at Maya. Her eyes widened.

"Uh-oh," said Maya. She shook her head. "I know that look," she teased Kat. "Trouble."

"No, not trouble," said Kat. "Maya, I have an idea."

"Exactly! See? Trouble!" said Maya, grinning. "Okay, Einstein. What is it?"

"What if we ask Aunt Jenn if we can help out with Bailey? Maybe she'll let us play with him!"

SUSAN HUGHES

Maya's eyes lit up. "Maybe she'd even let us feed him. Or walk him!"

Kat clapped her hands together. "Oh, Maya, wouldn't that be great?"

"I take it back. I think this is a great idea," said Maya.

"Aunt Jenn knows how much we love puppies. I'm sure she will let us play with Bailey," repeated Kat. "I just know it!"

CHAPTER 6

hen school ended for the day, Kat and Maya hurried to Tails Up!

"Wow, it's even busier than yesterday!" said Maya.

There were no empty chairs in the reception area. A red-haired woman sat with an Irish setter at her feet. An elderly man had two pugs on his lap. A young couple sat together with a basset hound puppy between them. A well-dressed woman with her legs crossed sat alone putting on lipstick and looking into a small compact mirror.

Kat and Maya were just deciding where
to stand and wait, when the door to the
grooming room opened. Out came Aunt

Jenn. She was being led by an exuberant Afghan hound.

"Oh, Portia. You look just wonderful!" cried the woman with newly red lips. The dog licked the woman's hand, her tail sweeping from side to side. "I am impressed, Jenn of Tails Up!" the woman said. She looked at her dog from one side and then the other. "I am very impressed. Portia and I will be back in eight weeks. I'll call to make an appointment. Until then." She handed Aunt Jenn some money and followed her eager Afghan hound out the door.

"Okeydokey," said Aunt Jenn. She wiped her brow. She smiled when she noticed Kat and Maya. She dropped the money into the cash register. Then she waved the girls toward the doggy day care room. She turned toward her customers. "Thank you for your patience," she said in her most professional voice. "I'll just be a moment."

As soon Aunt Jenn closed the door, she punched the air with her fist. "All right!" she cried. "Can you believe it, girls? It's day two, and there are people and dogs lined up to see me! Actual customers with actual dogs! Just like yesterday!"

"This is so great, Aunt Jenn!" Kat high-fived her aunt.

"It's terrific," said Maya.

Aunt Jenn grinned and did a little shimmy with her hips. Then she admitted, "But you know, Kitty-Kat, your dad was right. I'm swamped. I do need to get an assistant of some kind soon. Very soon! So, girls, we'll have to hang out another day, okay?" Aunt Jenn glanced at her watch. "I better get my next pooch in here, pronto."

"Okay, Aunt Jenn," Kat said. She glanced toward Bailey's crate. "But...well, how's Bailey? How's he doing?"

"He's fine," Aunt Jenn said. "Come on and see."

This time, the yellow Lab was awake. He yipped when he saw the girls approaching. His whole body wiggled as he wagged his tail.

"I've been in to see him several times today," said Aunt Jenn. "He still sleeps quite a bit because he's so young. But I think he might be a bit lonely."

"Oh, hello, Bailey-boy!" said Kat. She poked her fingers through the bars of the crate, and the puppy licked them enthusiastically.

Then Kat shot a look at Maya. Her friend gave her a nod and a thumbs-up.

Kat took a deep breath. "Aunt Jenn, can we ask you something? Something important?"

"Of course, Kat," Aunt Jenn replied. "What is it?"

"You know how much Maya and I both

love puppies," Kat began. "Do you think we could play with Bailey for a little while?"

For a moment, Aunt Jenn didn't say anything. She trained her blue eyes on the girls and studied them carefully. "Puppies are very cute," she said. "I couldn't agree more. But looking after them is a big responsibility. Dogs are very precious. And they are most precious to the people who love them best, their owners. When people bring their dogs here, they are putting a huge amount of trust in me. They need to know that they can count on me to keep their puppies safe and healthy."

Kat nodded, but she felt her heart sink.

Then Aunt Jenn went on. "But I do need help here. That's for certain. I'm a little busier than I thought I'd be!" She yanked out her ponytail and made a new, neater one. She straightened her white coat. "And Bailey could probably use a little more attention than I have been able to give him today."

Kat held her breath. Maya was still, waiting.

"So I'm going to agree to this," she said.

"Oh, Aunt Jenn! Thank you!" cried Kat. She felt Maya squeeze her hand, and she squeezed it back.

"This is to help Bailey, girls," Aunt Jenn reminded them. "You have to remember that he is not a toy. You need to make sure there's nothing he can chew on that will harm him. You must make sure you handle him gently and don't let him fall."

Aunt Jenn opened the door of Bailey's crate.

As she reached for the puppy, he began wiggling even more. He wanted out!

"You have to be very careful to hold him securely." Aunt Jenn showed them how to lift Bailey out of the crate. "Puppies are very wiggly, and they can easily wiggle right out of your grasp. As soon as you can, hold him against your own body. That will calm him and give you more control of his little squirmy body."

Aunt Jenn popped Bailey back in the crate. "Now, Kat, let me see you do it."

Kat felt a surge of happiness run through her. Carefully she opened the crate door and reached in. She lifted Bailey just as Aunt Jenn had shown her. She cupped one hand under his rear end and his back legs, and she used the other hand to grip his shoulders and front legs.

The puppy wriggled with joy, trying to climb up her arms.

Kat quickly pulled him close, hugging him against her chest. Bailey raised his head and licked her chin. Once, twice.

"Very good," said Aunt Jenn. She looked at her watch again. "Maya, your turn."

Kat put Bailey back in the crate, careful not to get his legs or tail caught on the opening. Then Maya practiced. She looked overjoyed to be holding the puppy.

"Well done! I think you've both got it. Now, today you can play with Bailey in this room only. Those are some of his toys," she said, pointing to a basket. Then she pointed to an area covered with newspaper. "This is where I am housebreaking Bailey. If you see him peeing or about to pee, please place him on the news-paper. Okay?" She headed to the door.

"Got it," said Maya.

"I'll be back in a bit," said Aunt Jenn. "Remember, don't take him outside. And come and get me if you need anything." Then she rushed back to her customers, and Kat and Maya were alone with the pup.

CHAPTER 7

"ello, little guy," Kat said softly. She patted the puppy's head. She touched his silk ears. Bailey squirmed and wiggled with delight in Maya's arms.

"Okay, let me put you down, Bailey," Maya said, struggling to hold the excited puppy. She squatted and gently set him on the floor.

Bailey sat on his haunches, smiling up at the girls.

"He's so tiny! Only eight weeks old," said

Kat. "I don't think I've ever seen a puppy so young before."

"Me either," agreed Maya.

"But look at his paws. They're huge!" Gently, Kat lifted one of Bailey's front paws. "That means you're going to be a big dog when you're fully grown," Kat told him.

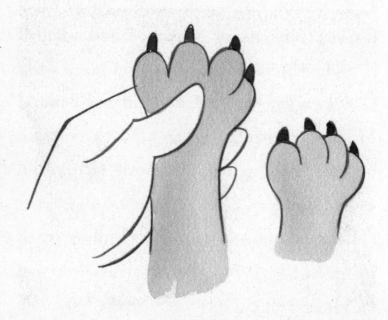

"Hey, do you think it's really true that retrievers have webbed feet?" asked Maya.

"Let's look," said Kat. She and Maya examined the bottom of Bailey's paw closely, spreading it gently.

"Hey, it really is webbed!" said Maya. "That is so cool!"

"I read that most dogs have a small amount of webbed skin between their toes but not enough to say they have webbed feet. But quite a few breeds do," Kat said. "Retrievers were bred to swim out to fishing nets and bring them back to shore, so the webbed feet help them to swim. That's what my *Dog Breeds of the World* says."

Restless, Bailey licked Kat's fingers, then pulled his paw away. He jumped to his feet and looked at the girls, wagging his tail.

"I think he wants to play!" said Maya.

"Good idea, Bailey," said Kat. "Let's do it!"

For almost an hour, the girls ran and tumbled with the puppy. He chased them, and then they chased him.

Round and round they went. Every once in a while, Bailey flopped down on his tummy and rested.

"Bailey has two speeds: full speed and full stop!" Kat told Maya, laughing.

Other times, the roly-poly puppy would go so fast, he'd lose his balance. He'd do a somersault, head over tail.

Finally, it was the girls' turn to catch their breath. Bailey bowed to them with both front paws out in front. It was as if he were saying, "Come on. Just try and get me!"

"We're taking a break, Bailey!" said Kat.

"Yeah, you're wearing us out!" Maya panted.

Bailey turned and sniffed the other empty crates. Then he found his big basket of toys. With a giant leap, he scrabbled over the side of the basket. He fell right into the jumble of rubber chew toys and cloth tug ropes. He twisted and turned until he was sitting again.

"Bailey, you're so cute!" Kat laughed.

Bailey grabbed a chew toy between his teeth. He shook it hard from side to side, his ears flying in all directions. Then he lost his balance and toppled over onto the toys again.

Maya giggled. "Oh, Kat, I wish I'd brought my camera! Oh, we could add Bailey's photo to our Puppy Collection!"

"Next time, for sure," agreed Kat.

"Kat, do you really think there will be a next time? Do you think your aunt will let us come and play with Bailey again tomorrow?" asked Maya wistfully.

"I sure hope so," said Kat. "Especially if we do a good job keeping Bailey happy today.

We'll prove to her that she can trust us and we can keep Bailey safe."

Just then Bailey leaped up. His ears swiveled here and there as he looked over the side of the basket. He waded through his toys to the side of the basket, attempting to climb over the side, when suddenly the whole basket tipped over. Everything tumbled out—all the toys and the puppy too!

"Oh, Bailey!" Kat cried in alarm. But the little yellow Lab picked himself up and gave an enormous shake. The girls both crouched down and clapped their hands.

"Good boy, Bailey!" they cried. "Here, boy!"

At once, Bailey's ears perked up and his eyes brightened. He galloped toward the girls at full puppy speed.

"Whoa, Bailey, slow down!" warned Kat. But Bailey came barreling toward them, and when he reached the girls, he couldn't stop. He tried, but his little legs went here and there. Bailey skidded into Kat, who fell back on her bum with a thump, knocking over Maya as well. Girls and puppy were tangled together in a heap.

Just then the door to the doggy day care opened.

"Aunt Jenn," cried Kat, her heart sinking. There was her aunt, frowning, her hands on her hips.

irls?" Aunt Jenn raised an eyebrow.

Kat and Maya jumped to their feet. Kat reached down and scooped up Bailey. "We're fine. Bailey's fine," Kat said quickly. "We were just playing. Everything's fine."

"Totally fine," Maya added.

Bailey gave a little happy puppy bark. He squirmed and licked Kat's hands. "See?" Kat said. "Bailey's fine."

Aunt Jenn's face cleared. She grinned. "Okay, that's good. I just thought I'd come and say thanks. It's probably time for Bailey to nap again. I'm sure you've tired him out! He'll be fine now until I close up and can spend the evening with him."

Kat nodded, hugging the sweet puppy close to her. Aunt Jenn wasn't angry. She wasn't worried about Bailey.

Carefully, Kat and Maya put Bailey back in his crate.

"Bye, little guy," Kat told him, giving him a last rub on the head.

"Have a good little sleep," said Maya. She kissed the palm of her hand and then placed the kiss onto the puppy's head.

"Thanks, girls," said Aunt Jenn. "It looks like you did a great job looking after Bailey today."

Kat and Maya held their breath. They didn't want to ask. They didn't dare hope. But they couldn't say good-bye until they knew.

"So," continued Aunt Jenn, "do you think you two could come again tomorrow and maybe Thursday afternoon as well? Bailey's owner won't be back until Thursday night. I'm sure Bailey would like some playmates, especially if I'm as busy tomorrow as I've been yesterday and today."

"We'd love to," said Kat. "Right, Maya?"

"You bet," agreed Maya with a huge smile on her face.

♡ ⚝ ◎

On Wednesday, the girls hurried toward Tails Up! right after school.

Kat complained to Maya as they walked. "Megan and Cora stood behind me in the line after recess. Then they started making little kissy noises as we walked back into class," said Kat. "When I turned around, they looked all innocent and said, 'Oh, Kat, were you look-ing for Owen?' They are so annoying. Can't they think of anything better to do than bug me?"

Maya shook her head. "I told you. Revenge. An eye for an eye. If they do something mean to you, do something mean back."

Kat shrugged. "Yeah, maybe," she said. And then all thoughts of school and Megan and Cora vanished as Kat turned onto Orchard Valley's main street. Tails Up! was in sight, and there was a little lonely puppy waiting for them.

Once again, the reception area was crowded with customers and their dogs. Kat was pleased. Aunt Jenn's business was doing so well!

The girls made a beeline to the doggy day care room.

"It's us, your buddies!" Kat called out to Bailey as they hurried toward his crate. She saw the puppy jump to his feet and wiggle. He gave little excited puppy woofs, asking to come out and play.

"I think Bailey recognizes us," cried Maya.

Kat lifted up the puppy and gave him the first hug. Then she passed him over to Maya, who covered his head in little kisses.

As soon as Maya set Bailey down, the retriever puppy went off to explore the room again, sniffing here and there, his tail high. After a while, the girls sat on the floor and rolled Bailey's ball back and forth between them. Bailey raced after it excitedly. The ball was too big for him to hold in his mouth, but he pounced on it like a kitten, and sometimes he managed to trap it between his big puppy paws. The girls laughed while he wrestled with it.

The golden-yellow puppy had tons of energy, but Kat and Maya were careful to make sure he didn't get into any mischief. He even used his newspaper properly!

Dinnertime came quickly. It was time to put Bailey back in his crate.

Kat picked him up and snuggled him in

her arms, enjoying his puppy smell. The girls stood in the sunshine, looking out the window at the backyard.

The yard was large and surrounded by a chain-link fence. There was a smaller fenced area along one side, something like a doggy "playpen." There were also some bushes and trees running down two sides of the fence for shade.

Kat pointed at a small children's wading pool propped up against the fence. "I bet Aunt Jenn is going to fill that with water for her boarders one day," she said.

Reluctantly, the girls said good-bye to Bailey. Kat gave the weary puppy a final kiss on the head, and Maya tugged gently on his ears. "We'll see you again tomorrow, little guy," Maya said.

"Don't worry; we'll be back," Kat said, putting him back in the crate.

"Maybe we should take Bailey outside tomorrow," Maya suggested as the girls headed home. "I bet he'd love playing on the grass."

"He would," Kat agreed. "And imagine how much fun he'd have splashing around in the pool."

"Well then, let's do it," Maya said. "Let's take him in the back tomorrow."

Kat shook her head. "Aunt Jenn said we had to stay inside with him, remember?"

"Well, at least let's think about it, okay?" she suggested. "It would be for Bailey, after all. His last afternoon with us."

CHAPTER 9

All day Thursday, Kat had trouble concentrating on her work. She usually daydreamed about puppies, dozens of them in all sizes and colors. But today there was only one puppy in her thoughts: Bailey.

And the only thing she kept picturing was how much fun Bailey would have outside in the Tails Up! yard. She imagined him rolling in the grass and sniffing at all the outdoor smells. She imagined him free to run full speed from one end of the yard to the other, his ears flying out.

SUSAN HUGHES

"Kat, are you with us?" asked her teacher.

"Yes, Ms. Mitchell," said Kat, returning to her math problem.

After lunch, it was even worse. The afternoon went so slowly! When the class was supposed to be working on their stories, Kat found it impossible to keep her mind off Bailey. She couldn't wait to hear his little woofs when he saw her and Maya. She couldn't wait to stroke his silky head and tickle his tummy. And the yard? Maybe she would ask Aunt Jenn if she and Maya could take him outside, just for a few minutes.

Kat kept looking at the clock. The more often she looked, the slower the hands seemed to move.

Then Heather, who sat behind her, passed

her a note. "Dreaming about Owen?" the note asked. It had little pink hearts all around it.

Of course, she knew right away who had written it. She looked over at Megan and Cora. The two girls were watching her, their hands over their mouths, giggling.

Angrily, Kat crumpled up the note in her hand.

Then Ms. Mitchell was crouching beside her chair. "Something on your mind today?" she asked Kat gently.

Kat saw the expression on Megan's and Cora's faces change. Now they looked scared.

"Yes," she said, nodding. She held the note in the palm of her hand. It would be so easy to show it to Ms. Mitchell. It might finally stop Megan and Cora from teasing her.

"Do you want to tell me about it? Are you missing Maya?" Ms. Mitchell asked.

Kat paused. Maya. It was Maya who had suggested she take revenge on the two girls. Telling Ms. Mitchell about the note would serve them right. They'd probably have to stay in after school. Or they'd have to help out in the kindergarten classrooms at lunchtime. Something.

"Kat?" Ms. Mitchell asked.

Kat wanted to make the girls squirm. But she also she didn't want to be a tattletale. It wasn't like they were bullying her. Not really. And she hadn't even tried telling them to stop.

Kat made up her mind. "My aunt opened her dog boarding and grooming place in town," she told her teacher. "And I'm helping her by looking after a puppy after school today. His name is Bailey."

"I've seen your aunt's sign. Tails Up!, right?" Ms. Mitchell asked.

"That's it!" said Kat, her face lighting up.

"Hmmm... That sounds really exciting." Ms. Mitchell knew how much Kat loved puppies. Everyone in the whole school seemed to know! "I have an idea. Since you're supposed to be working on a story now, why don't you write a story about Bailey? That way you can think about him and do your work, all at the same time?"

"Okay," said Kat, giving her teacher a smile. "I'll try that."

She picked up her pencil, and right away the words began pouring out. She didn't give Megan and Cora another thought.

CHAPTER 10

After school, Kat waited outside for Maya. When Owen walked past, Kat saw a baseball fall from his pocket.

"Owen, you dropped your ball," Kat said, picking it up for him.

Just then, Megan and Cora walked by. "Kat and Owen, sitting in a tree," Megan chanted.

Cora started to join in, but Kat had had enough.

"That's it!" she yelled. The girls were surprised. They stopped and looked at her.

"I didn't tell on you in class today. But I

still have the note. You need to leave me alone. Owen is *not* my boyfriend," Kat said.

She looked at Owen. His face was completely red, and he looked very embarrassed. She hoped she hadn't hurt his feelings.

"But he is my friend," Kat added. "And you need to leave him alone too."

"We were only having fun," Cora said.

"Yeah," said Megan. "You don't have to be so sensitive! Come on, Cora, let's go."

Megan and Cora stomped off across the schoolyard. Kat was shaking. They'd made her so mad!

"I was tired of them bugging me too," Owen said. "Do you think they'll stop now?"

"I think they just pick on us because we're quiet. Now that we stood up to them, they might leave us alone," said Kat. "And if not, I have proof they've been teasing us. They sent me a note." She smiled and patted her pocket.

"Hi, Kat! Hi, Owen!" Maya walked up and beamed at them both.

"Hi, Maya," Owen mumbled, looking at his

shoes. "Um, I'd better get going. See you, Kat. And thanks."

As Owen left, Maya turned to Kat. Her eyes were big. "What was that about?" she asked.

Kat told her friend about the note Cora and Megan had sent her in class. Then she told her how she'd stood up to them.

"Wow, that's awesome, Kat!" Maya said. "I bet they leave you alone now."

"I hope so. Anyway, we'd better get to Tails Up! Bailey's owner is coming tonight. We don't want to miss him!"

"Good idea," said Maya.

The girls watched Bailey as he investigated one

of the empty crates in the doggy day care room. He tilted his head to one side then the other. Now he put his front paws up on the side of the crate and tried to climb on top. The girls giggled as he toppled over, then bounded up and tried again.

Suddenly Maya said, "Oh, I brought my camera!" She ran to her backpack and got it

out. "Now we can add Bailey to our Puppy Collection!"

"Good thinking!" said Kat. "Hey, maybe we can add the story I wrote about Bailey too."

"Yeah!" said Maya. "I can't wait to read it."

Maya started snapping shots of Bailey tackling the crate. Kat threw a chew toy for the puppy, and Maya took more photos of Bailey playing with it. When Bailey grew tired of the toy, Kat played chase with him around and around the room. Maya took even more shots.

Then she paused. "It would be so great if we could take Bailey out in the sunshine," she said. "I know we can't," she added hurriedly. "But wouldn't it be fun?"

"He'd love it," Kat agreed. "Playing on the grass."

"Smelling the bushes and trees," said Maya.

For a moment neither girl said anything.

"I could ask Aunt Jenn," said Kat.

She looked out the window. It was another beautiful day, but it was getting close to dinnertime.

"I'll be right back," she told Maya. She hurried out of the room and into the reception area. A woman with a shaggy sheepdog was speaking to Aunt Jenn. It was almost impossible to tell the front of the dog from the back!

"Not too short, but I don't want the hair left too long either," the woman said. "Alice prefers it that way."

As the woman bent down to pat her dog, Aunt Jenn looked at Kat over her head and widened her eyes crazily. Kat couldn't help giggling.

"Okay, I think I have the right idea," Aunt Jenn said, trying to interrupt. But the woman wasn't done yet. Kat had the feeling she'd been speaking for quite some time.

"Alice is nine years old," the woman said, "and she is quite particular about her hairstyles."

"I see, I see," Aunt Jenn interrupted politely. "Well, let's take Alice into the grooming room, and I'll get her settled while you continue." She slowly guided the woman and her dog toward the grooming room. As she went, she shot Kat another kooky look and mouthed, "Help me!"

"She's too busy," Kat told Maya, returning to the doggy day care room. "I couldn't speak with her."

"Okay, well," said Maya. She was holding Bailey. "What do you think we should do?"

The girls went over to the window and looked outside.

"Your aunt told us not to take Bailey outside, but that was two days ago. That was on the first day we played with Bailey," Maya reminded

Kat. "She probably wasn't sure yet if we were responsible. She was just trying us out."

"Yeah," Kat agreed.

"I bet if you'd asked her now, she would have said yes," Maya said.

"Yeah, maybe," Kat said.

A squirrel searched for food in the back garden, twitching its tail. *What would Bailey do if he saw a squirrel?* Kat wondered. It made her smile.

"Hey, what did the tree wear to the pool party?" Kat asked Maya.

Maya grinned. "I don't know. What did the tree wear to the pool party?"

"Swimming trunks," said Kat.

Maya groaned loudly. "Not funny," she said.

The girls watched as the squirrel ran up the

side of the fence and jumped onto a tree branch. Bailey's ears pricked up.

"You saw that squirrel too, didn't you, Bailey?" Maya asked with a laugh.

"The backyard looks pretty safe," Kat said. "There's a fence all the way around it. I doubt Bailey could get into trouble back there." She patted the puppy's head. "What do you think, Bailey? Do you want to go outside?" The puppy began to squirm and whine. Kat and Maya laughed.

"You do want to go outside, don't you, Bailey?" Kat said. "We thought so!"

"What if we take him outside for only a few minutes? Five minutes. We'll time it," said Maya. She showed Kat her wristwatch. "Should we?"

Kat and Maya stared at each other. Should

they do it, even though Aunt Jenn had said not to? She'd placed a lot of trust in them. She'd even let them come back and help again because they'd done such a good job the first day. They'd been responsible and taken very good care of Bailey. Then again, how could going in the backyard possibly hurt the puppy? It would be so much fun for him. Should they?

CHAPTER 11

Suddenly, at exactly the same moment, both girls made up their minds. They blurted out, "No!"

Then they burst out laughing because they'd surprised each other, speaking at exactly the same time, saying exactly the same thing.

Just then, Aunt Jenn came bursting through the door. She was clutching her stomach.

"What happened, Aunt Jenn?" cried Kat. She placed Bailey in Maya's arms and rushed over to her aunt. "Is everything okay? Why aren't you grooming Alice?" she asked, putting her arm around Aunt Jenn's shoulders.

"Oh, girls, some dog people are so funny! Just so funny!" Aunt Jenn's shoulders were shaking. Kat realized her aunt was laughing!

"Alice's owner decided to book an appointment for a different day. She just felt Alice was not in the right emotional state of mind to be clipped today," Aunt Jenn spluttered. "Especially by a groomer who she'd never met." She put her hand to her chest. "Oh my," she gasped. "Oh my."

Kat and Maya started to laugh along with her.

Then the girls suddenly had the same horrible thought. What if they had gone outside just now? Aunt Jenn would have seen them! What would she have said? What would she have done? Right away, they knew they'd been right to follow Aunt Jenn's directions.

"You came out to speak to me a few minutes ago, Kat. Was there something you wanted?" Aunt Jenn asked.

Kat blushed. "No, not really, Aunt Jenn." Then she added in a rush, "Other than, we just wanted to say thanks for letting us help out with Bailey, and we hope his owner is pleased that she boarded him here."

Aunt Jenn came over and patted Bailey's head. He looked up at her with his blue eyes and smiled.

"Well, girls, there were two things I wanted to tell you. First of all, there's good news about the backyard. I have someone coming to fix the holes in the fence this weekend. You can't

see them from here, but there are several large openings behind those trees. A puppy could wiggle under the fence and be gone in a flash! But once the fence is fixed, we can exercise the dogs back there."

Aunt Jenn had said "we"! Kat swallowed hard but didn't say anything. Maya clutched her arm hard.

"And the second thing: you've really proven yourselves to me. You've done a fine job following instructions and being so good to Bailey. I hope that you'll be able to help me out on a regular basis. Even if I do get an assistant, and—I know, I know, I need to do that…" She waved her hands around. "Anyway, I wanted to check with you first to make sure you could continue to come and give me a hand."

Kat and Maya beamed. "We've love to," Maya cried.

"Thanks so much for asking!" said Kat.

"Well then, it's a deal. Okay, well, I have to get back to the next customer. A supercute little pug that needs his nails clipped," Aunt Jenn said. "I'll see you soon, right, girls?"

"Right, Aunt Jenn," Kat and Maya said.

As soon as the door closed behind the groomer, Kat and Maya stared at each other.

"Can you imagine if we'd gone outside with this little guy and he'd escaped?" Kat whispered. "You would have found one of those holes, wouldn't you, Bailey? You're so clever and such an explorer." She reached out and rubbed his tummy.

"You might have got lost. You might have got hurt…" Maya said softly. Bailey lifted his head and licked her chin.

"And Aunt Jenn never would have trusted us again!" said Kat.

For a moment, the girls didn't speak, and then smiles swept across their faces. "Kat," Maya said. "We get to come and help out at Tails Up! all the time!"

"And we'll have lots more puppies to add to our Puppy Collection!" cried Kat.

"Let's play with Bailey a little bit more before we say good-bye to him," said Maya, setting the squirmy golden-yellow puppy back down on the floor.

Immediately, he bounded across the floor toward his knotted rope toy. He grabbed it between his teeth and shook it. Then he threw it up in the air. When it dropped, he ran and pounced on it and shook it between his teeth again.

The girls laughed in delight. They had a real live puppy to add to their collection!

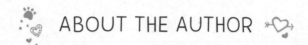# ABOUT THE AUTHOR

Award-winning author Susan Hughes has written over thirty books—both fiction and nonfiction—for children of all ages, including *Earth to Audrey, Island Horse, Four Seasons of Patrick, Off to Class: Incredible and Unusual Schools around the World,* and *Case Closed? Nine Mysteries Unlocked by Modern Science.* She is also a freelance editor and writing coach. Susan lives with her family in Toronto, Canada, in a house with a big red door—and wishes it could always be summer. You can visit her at susanhughes.ca.

Kat and Maya's
PUPPY ADVENTURES
continue with
RILEY,
a loving golden retriever puppy!

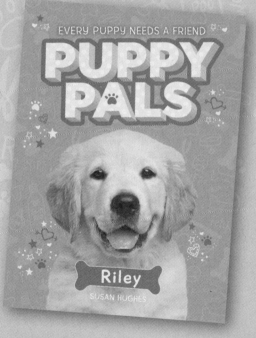

WATCH OUT FOR MORE PUPPY PALS BOOKS FEATURING MANY OTHER ADORABLE PUPPIES!